AEROTITAN

JAINOSAURUS

UTAHRAPTOR

GUALICHO

JIANGJUNOSAURUS

AUSTRORAPTOR

ATACAMATITAN

ANCHICERATOPS

LABOCANIA

MASSOSPONDYLUS

JANE YOLEN

How Do Dinosaurs Say Trick Or Treat?

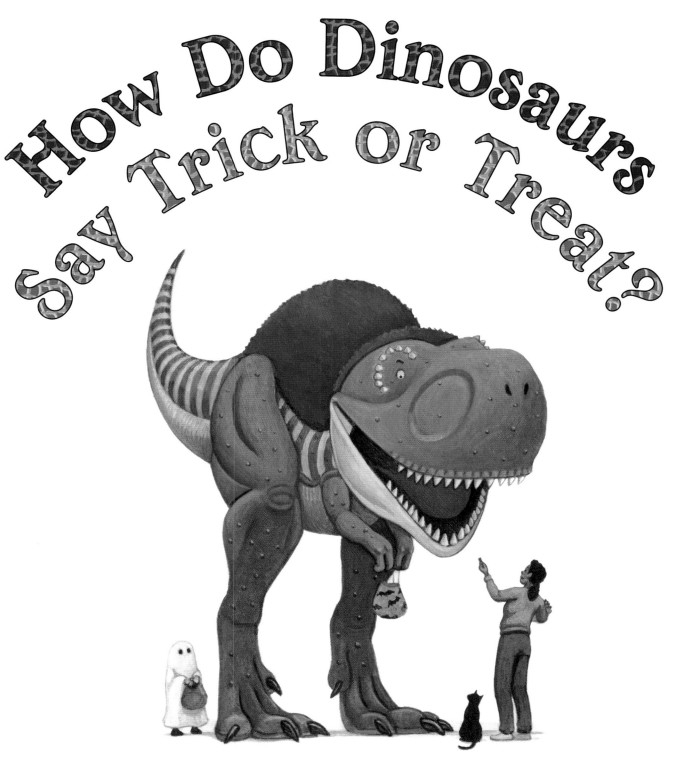

Illustrated by
MARK TEAGUE

SCHOLASTIC PRESS • NEW YORK

For M.T. — J.Y.

For Lulabelle and Guillermo — M.T.

Library of Congress Cataloging-in-Publication Data available
ISBN 978-1-338-89198-0
10 9 8 7 6 5 4 3 2 1   24 25 26 27 28

Printed in China 38
First edition, July 2024

How does a dinosaur say
"trick or treat"
When walking with kids
on a Halloween street?

Does he bang on the door
with his very strong tail?

Does he stomp on the pumpkins
and throw around bits?

Does he fear he will slip and
then slide into splits?

How does a dinosaur say
"trick or treat" . . .

. . . when she skips down the path on her extra-large feet?

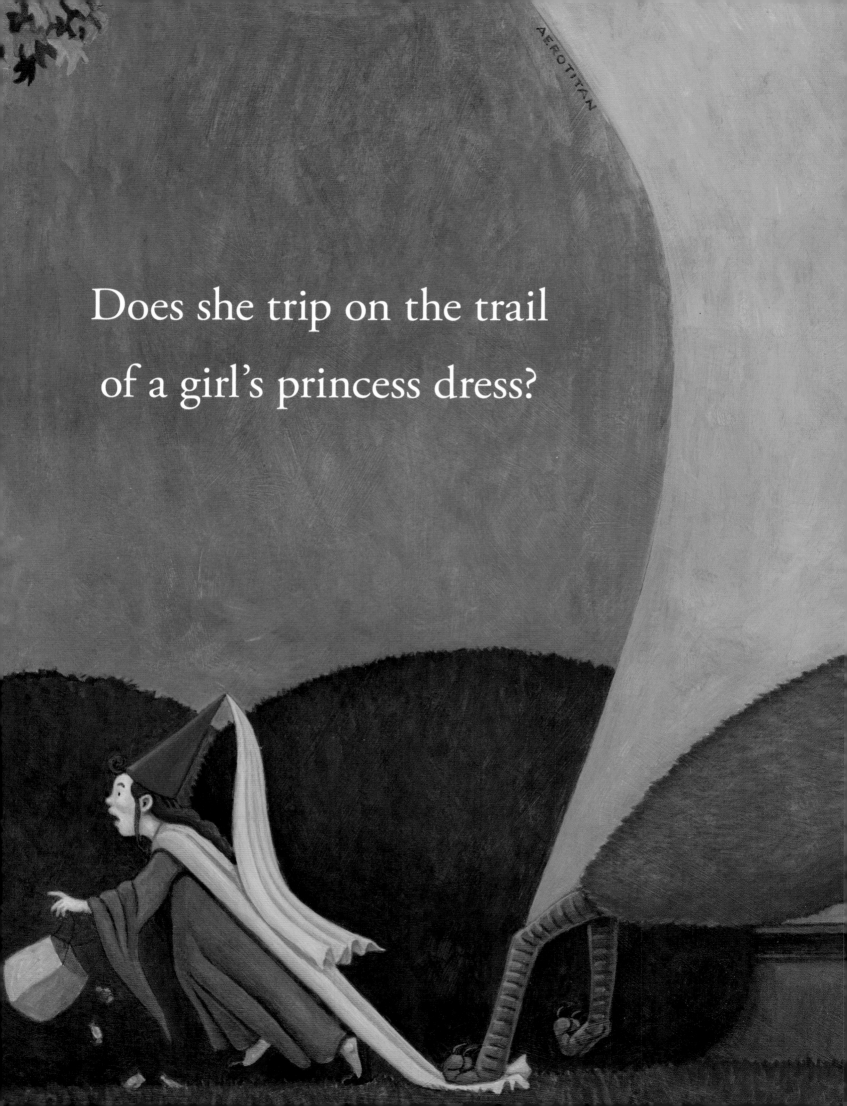

Does she trip on the trail
of a girl's princess dress?

Does she grab for
more treats and then
make a big mess?

Do they shout "Boo" to parents
who watch from the side?

Do they scream

"TRICK OR TREAT!!!!"

with their mouths opened wide?

Do they run around madly or stomp on the ground?

Do they turn the treats

into a towering mound?

NO . . . DINOSAURS DON'T . . .

It's a big point of pride:

Free treats

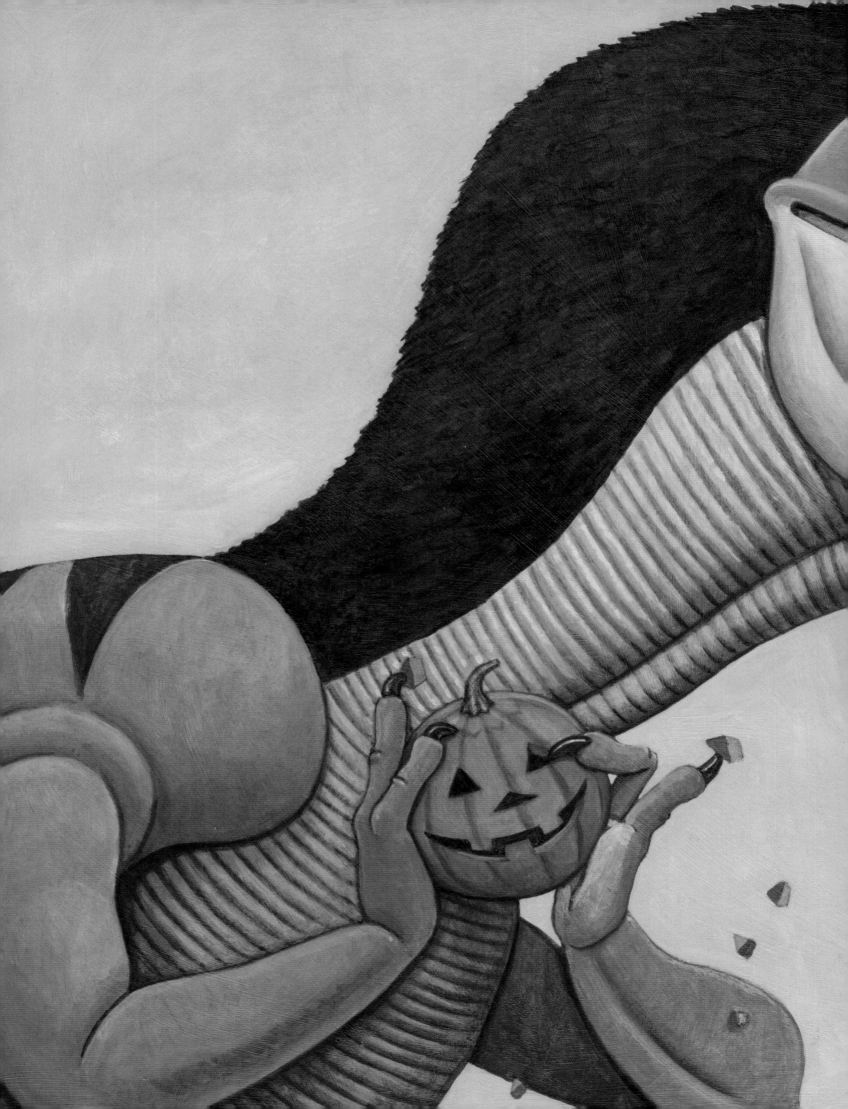

They carve all the pumpkins

to make the smiles wide.

They help little witches to carry their brooms.

And they hand out awards for
the scariest costumes.

And they are the ones who
open each door.

Trick or treat —

YOU'RE the sweet,

my dear dinosaur.

AEROTITAN

JAINOSAURUS

UTAHRAPTOR

GUALICHO

AUSTRORAPTOR

ATACAMATITAN

JIANGJUNOSAURUS

ANCHICERATOPS

LABOCANIA

MASSOSPONDYLUS